BEATRICE DOESN'T WANT TO

BEATRICE
DOESN'T
WANT TO

by
Laura Joffe Numeroff

An Easy-Read Story Book

Franklin Watts
New York/London/Toronto/Sydney
1981

Library of Congress Cataloging in Publication Data

Numeroff, Laura Joffe.
  Beatrice doesn't want to.

  (An Easy-read story book)
  SUMMARY: Beatrice doesn't like books or li-
braries until on one forced visit to the library with
her brother she discovers the children's room.
  [1. Books and reading—Fiction. 2. Libraries—
Fiction] I. Title.
PZ7.N964Be   [E]   81-447
ISBN 0-531-03537-9   AACR1
ISBN 0-531-04299-5 (lib. bdg.)

R.L. 2.0 Spache Revised Formula

For Kelly... January First, Nineteen Eighty

Beatrice didn't like books.
She didn't even like to read.
More than that, she hated going to
the library.

But that's where her brother Henry
had to take her three afternoons in
a row.
He had to write a report on dinosaurs.
Mother was busy and Henry had to
look after Beatrice.

"Why don't you get some books from
the shelf," Henry suggested when they
got to the library.
"I don't want to," Beatrice said.
"Look at how many books there are!"
Henry tried.
"I don't want to," Beatrice repeated.

"Then what do you want to do?" Henry
asked her.
"I want to watch you," she said.
"But I have to work," said Henry.
"I'll watch."

"I give up," said Henry.
He worked on his report.
Beatrice watched.
Henry tried not to notice her.

The second day, Beatrice didn't even
want to go inside.
"Come on, Bea," Henry said.
"I don't want to," Beatrice told him.
"But I have to work."

"I'll just sit outside," Beatrice decided.
"OK," said Henry. "But don't move until
I come out."
Beatrice promised.

Henry went inside to do his report.
All of a sudden, he felt drops of water.
He didn't know where they were
coming from.
Then he felt someone tap his
shoulder.

Henry turned around, and there was
Beatrice.
She was soaking wet.
"It's raining," she said.
"I give up," said Henry.

It was still raining the third day.

Beatrice *had* to go inside this time.

She followed Henry around while he looked for more books.
"Can I hold some?" Beatrice asked.
Henry gave her some books to hold.

"They're too heavy," Beatrice wailed.
The books dropped onto her foot, and
she began to cry.
"I really do give up!" said Henry. "You
are driving me crazy!" He glared at her.

"Look, Bea, I've got to get this report
done. It's due tomorrow. Please!"
Henry begged her.
"Henry," said Beatrice, "do
you think I could have a drink of water?"

And they went down a hall to look for some water.

Suddenly Henry saw a poster.
This was it!

"Come on," said Henry.
"I don't want to," answered Beatrice.
"That's too bad!" shouted Henry.

Before Beatrice knew it, she was in a
room full of boys and girls.
Henry walked out just as she started
to say "I don't want—"

"Hello. My name is Wanda. This is the
second time I've heard this story,"
said the girl in the next chair.
"Big deal!" said Beatrice.

"Alfred Mouse lived in a brand new house," the librarian began to read. She held the book up so everyone could see the pictures.
Beatrice glared out the window.

"Alfred Mouse also had new roller
skates," the librarian continued.
Beatrice loved to roller skate.
She looked at the librarian.

"But Alfred's mother wasn't too thrilled
when he skated through the house,"
the librarian read.
The boys and girls laughed.
Beatrice smiled.

She remembered the time she had
tried roller skating in her own house.
Then Beatrice laughed.
She listened to the whole story.

When the story was over, Beatrice
went up to the librarian.
"May I see that book, please?" she
asked.
"Of course," said the librarian.

Beatrice sat down and looked at each
picture over and over.

Suddenly she felt someone tapping her shoulder.
"Time to go," Henry whispered in her ear.
Beatrice kept looking at the pictures.

Henry stuck Beatrice's hat on her
head.
"We have to go home now," he said.
Beatrice ignored him.
"Come on, Bea," Henry said.

"I don't want to," Beatrice said.